When I Go Camping with Grandma

by Marion Dane Bauer   Illustrated by Allen Garns

BridgeWater Paperback

Text copyright © 1995 by Marion Dane Bauer.

Illustrations copyright © 1995 by Allen Garns.

Published by BridgeWater Paperback, an imprint and trademark of
Troll Communications L.L.C.

First published in hardcover by BridgeWater Books.

First paperback edition 1996.

Printed in the United States of America.

10 9 8 7 6 5 4 3 2 1

Library of Congress Cataloging-in-Publication Data

Bauer, Marion Dane.
When I go camping with Grandma / by Marion Dane Bauer;
pictures by Allen Garns.
p.   cm.
Summary: A child enjoys a camping trip with Grandma that
includes hiking, canoeing, fishing, and cooking out.
ISBN 0-8167-3448-8 (lib.)   ISBN 0-8167-3449-6 (pbk.)
[1. Camping—Fiction.   2. Grandmothers—Fiction.]
I. Garns, Allen, ill.   II. Title.
PZ7.B3262Wh   1995   [E]—dc20   93-33809

For my grandchildren,

those who are and those who are yet to come.

M.D.B.

To my father,

who taught me to love the outdoors.

A.G.

When I go camping with Grandma, we hike deep into the woods. Grandma holds my hand and sings to scare away the bears.

She builds a fire, and we roast hot dogs until they sputter and split. Juice dribbles down our chins when we eat.

A marshmallow on a stick grows fat and brown. Quick! Catch it!

Grandma paddles the canoe through sunlight spread on black water. "I used to have a silk dress that looked just like this," she says.

Tree bones stand in the lake. We drop our hooks and wait. Shhhh!

A heron wings over our heads. Great blue shadow. Pterodactyl.

The sun grows flat and red. It dips into the edge of the lake.

And a fish comes shining, gasping into the air.
"Shall we have fish for breakfast?" Grandma asks.
"You know I like pancakes," I remind her.

She slips the fish off the hook and into the water.
It lies still, waiting. Then it flicks its tail and is gone
in a wiggle of light.

We climb into our sleeping bags, whisper in the dark.

"Good night."

"Good night."

"Good night," I say again.

In the morning I pop my head out of the tent.
The moon floats low in the bluing sky like a
balloon left from a night party.

A squirrel nibbles a marshmallow.
A gauzy hammock in the grass holds a spider's
breakfast and a sip of dew.

"Wake up, Grandma," I call. "The day is here."
Grandma yawns, stretches, rubs her eyes. "Dear
me," she says, "the ground is hard. Maybe my bones
are getting too old for camping."

We look at each other for a long time. Then we laugh and hug.

Soon I'll be taller, stronger. I'll sing away the bears when we hike in the woods. I'll build the fire and paddle the canoe. And when Grandma catches a fish, I'll slip it off the hook. And together we'll watch it wiggle away into the black silk water.